# The Creepy Sleep-Over

## Beverly Lewis

# Beverly Lewis Books for Young Readers

## PICTURE BOOK

*Cows in the House*

## THE CUL-DE-SAC KIDS

*The Double Dabble Surprise*
*The Chicken Pox Panic*
*The Crazy Christmas Angel Mystery*
*No Grown-ups Allowed*
*Frog Power*
*The Mystery of Case D. Luc*
*The Stinky Sneakers Mystery*
*Pickle Pizza*
*Mailbox Mania*
*The Mudhole Mystery*
*Fiddlesticks*
*The Crabby Cat Caper*
*Tarantula Toes*
*Green Gravy*
*Backyard Bandit Mystery*
*Tree House Trouble*
*The Creepy Sleep-Over*
*The Great TV Turn-Off*

*Mountain Bikes and Garbanzo Beans*
*The Six-Hour Mystery*
*Mystery at Midnight*
*Katie and Jake and the Haircut Mistake*

# THE CUL-DE-SAC KIDS

# The Creepy Sleep-Over

## Beverly Lewis

# BETHANY HOUSE PUBLISHERS
## MINNEAPOLIS, MINNESOTA 55438

*The Creepy Sleep-Over*
Copyright © 1998
Beverly Lewis

Cover illustration by Paul Turnbaugh
Text illustrations by Janet Huntington

Published by Bethany House Publishers
A Ministry of Bethany Fellowship, Inc.
11300 Hampshire Avenue South
Minneapolis, Minnesota 55438

Printed in the United States of America by
Bethany Press International, Minneapolis, Minnesota 55438

**Library of Congress Cataloging-in-Publication Data**

Lewis, Beverly, 1949–
    The creepy sleep-over / by Beverly Lewis.
      p.   cm. — (The cul-de-sac kids ; 17)
    Summary: Dunkum tries to hide his fear from the other Cul-de-sac Kids when they spend the night at their teacher's house.
    ISBN 1–55661–988–X (pbk.)
    [1.  Sleep-overs—Fiction.  2.  Fear—Fiction.
3.  Teachers—Fiction.  4.  Christian life—Fiction.]  I.  Title.
II.  Series: Lewis, Beverly, 1949–      Cul-de-sac kids ; 17
PZ7.L58464Cre     1997
[Fic]dc21                          97–33925
                                          CIP
                                          AC

For
Peggy Littleton's first grade class
at
Colorado Springs Christian
Elementary School

| | |
|---|---|
| Patrick Antrim | Luke Nelson |
| Brooke Humphreys | Rebecca Glisan |
| Julia Bennett | Chelsea Samelson |
| Kirsten Kruger | Eric Goldberg |
| Matthew Fenlason | Marielle Sheppel |
| Amanda Lenehan | Mark Hernandez |
| Adam Fekula | P.Y. Young |
| Cole Moberly | Carisa Hoogenboom |
| Conner Fitzgerald | Blake Wittenberg |
| Christopher Murphy | Jessica Hollingsworth |
| Brynden Flick | Aide: Sue Obenauf |

THE CUL-DE-SAC KIDS

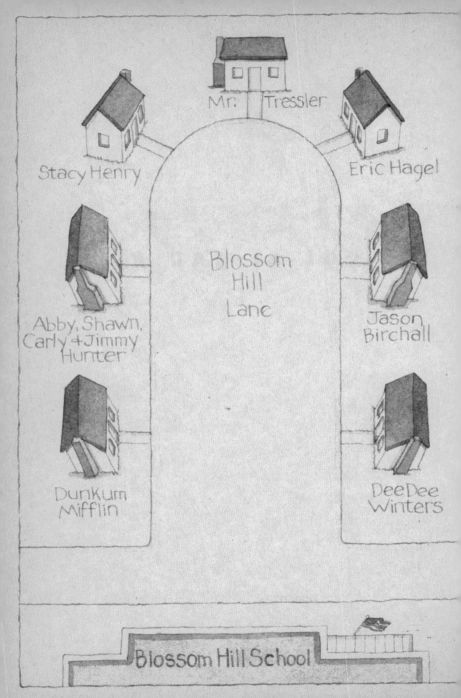

# ONE

It was a super Saturday.

Dunkum Mifflin was jumpin' happy. He slam-dunked his basketball. Three times in a row! *Hoo-ray!*

His name was on Miss Hershey's reading list. He'd checked it twice. He'd made his reading goal. Twenty-five books in all!

The reward was a sleep-over at the teacher's house. Eight kids from Miss Hershey's class were going.

They'd eat pizza and junk food. And ice-cream sundaes and root-beer floats.

Best of all, they were spending the night!

Eric Hagel and Jason Birchall arrived at Dunkum's house. They passed the ball around. They talked about the sleep-over.

"Where's Miss Hershey's house, anyway?" Dunkum asked.

Jason didn't know exactly.

Eric didn't, either. "She used to be on my paper route. But not anymore," he said.

"Did she move?" Dunkum asked.

Eric scratched his head. "Guess so."

"Somewhere out in the country," Jason piped up. "I heard it's a haunted mansion!"

"How do you know?" Dunkum asked.

Eric and Jason laughed. "Everyone says so," replied Eric.

"*Everyone?*" Dunkum said.

"Well, you know." Jason crossed his eyes. "It's gonna be such a cool sleep-over. Even if the house *is* haunted."

Eric agreed. "I still can't believe it. Did I really read all those books?"

Jason grinned. "Your name's on Miss Hershey's list, right?"

Eric nodded and passed the ball to Dunkum.

Dunkum shot up . . . up . . . *whoosh!* "Anyone else going from our cul-de-sac?"

"Abby and Stacy are," Eric replied.

"Abby oughta be going. She read over *fifty* books," Jason said.

"Wow! How'd she do it?" Dunkum asked.

"She's a bookworm. That's how." Eric laughed.

Dunkum was thrilled. Most of his friends were going to the sleep-over.

"I heard Miss Hershey tells bedtime stories," Eric said. "Spooky ones."

"Yeah, better watch out," Jason warned.

"How come?" Dunkum asked.

"She likes stuff by Edgar Allen Poe,"

said Eric. "Every year, same thing."

"Who's this Poe dude?" asked Dunkum.

Jason started laughing. "Edgar Allen Poe wrote mystery stories and poems. Ever hear of 'The Raven'? It's famous."

"Nope," Dunkum said.

"Well, you'll hear it plenty," Eric said.

Jason flapped his arms. "Sounds wingy-dingy. Get it? Ravens have wings—"

"Aw . . . Jason, act your age," Dunkum scolded.

"Whatever," Jason muttered and stopped flying around.

The boys shot some more baskets. "How do *you* know about the sleep-over?" Dunkum asked Eric.

"Miss Hershey has one every year. The kids from last year's class told me." Eric's voice was low and quiet. "They told me ALL about it."

Dunkum hoped the sleep-over wasn't

too scary. He wasn't a scaredy-cat or any-thing. He just didn't like creepy things.

Jason interrupted his thoughts. "You're not afraid of haunted mansions, are you?" He made his voice sound spooky. "Ooooooooooow!" he squealed.

"You don't scare me!" Dunkum said.

"But Miss Hershey will," teased Jason.

Dunkum dribbled the ball hard. He leaped up and dunked it. That's how he got his nickname—Dunkum. His real name was Edward. But nobody called him that. He was Dunkum—the tallest and best hoop shooter around.

Dunkum thought hard as he aimed the basketball. Jason could say all he wanted. But their teacher was the best. She wouldn't plan a creepy sleep-over.

No way. Dunkum didn't believe it for one second!

# TWO

It was Friday morning.

Heavy snow was falling. First storm of the New Year.

Miss Hershey's class was all bunched up. Their teeth chattered as they huddled near the outside door.

Dunkum was glad for his heavy jacket. "Tonight's the sleep-over at Miss Hershey's house," he said.

"Maybe we'll get snowed in," Jason said.

Abby grinned. "I wouldn't mind. I heard about Miss Hershey's old house,"

15

she said. "She has eight cats. And she likes Mozart—played in a minor key. Perfect for a haunted mansion, you know."

*Sounds like a haunted cat shelter*, thought Dunkum.

The first bell rang. Miss Hershey's classroom door swung open. She greeted the students. "Hurry, hurry, children. Come in where it's warm."

Dunkum liked her cheerful voice. She was saying things his mom might say on a cold day. He watched her smiling face.

She was cool. Really, *really* cool! Miss Hershey couldn't possibly live in a haunted mansion.

Could she?

★ ★ ★

The teacher wrote the date on the board. *January 19*.

"Today is a famous person's birthday," she said. "Does anyone know who?"

Abby Hunter raised her hand.

"Yes, Abby?"

"It's Edgar Allen Poe's birthday. He was born in 1809," Abby recited.

Dunkum's hand shot up.

"Yes, Dunkum?" said Miss Hershey.

"Poe was a *mystery* writer." Dunkum grinned. He was glad Eric and Jason had filled him in earlier.

Miss Hershey nodded and smiled. "That's right. Poe was born almost two hundred years ago today."

Dunkum listened as Miss Hershey told about Edgar Allan Poe. "He was an American poet. A short story writer, too," she said.

Dunkum liked short stories. He'd even written a few himself.

"Poe's works are almost like music," said Miss Hershey.

Dunkum had never heard such a thing. He'd read tons of books. Lots of them! But he'd never found tunes hidden

17

in the words or sentences.

He didn't get it. What did Miss Hershey mean?

★  ★  ★

By recess, the ground was covered white. But the snow had stopped.

Some of the Cul-de-sac Kids made a fort. Abby and Stacy helped pack down the snow.

Dunkum and Jason carried armfuls of white wet stuff.

Eric and Shawn made little cannon-balls out of snow.

Dunkum kept thinking about Miss Hershey's house. "Why does she live in a mansion?" he asked Eric.

"She's weird, that's why," Eric said.

"How can you say that?" Dunkum replied.

"Well, she lives with a bunch of cats. No husband, no kids," Jason chimed in. "Isn't that kinda weird?"

"So what? Not everyone gets married," Eric said.

Dunkum knew that was true. His mother's cousin was almost forty and still single.

*Whoosh!* He plopped down a pile of snow near the fort. "Being single's not weird." Dunkum sighed. "I wanna know why she lives in a mansion."

"Maybe she's rich," Abby spoke up.

Stacy shook her head. "I doubt it."

"How come?" Dunkum asked.

"Teachers don't make much money. Besides, she doesn't dress rich," Stacy said.

"No diamond rings or bracelets," added Abby.

Dunkum thought about that. "Miss Hershey dresses real pretty, though."

"And her hair's always perfect," Abby said.

"Maybe she gives her money away . . . to poor kids," Dunkum said.

19

"Hey! *I'm* poor," Jason laughed. He twirled his glasses around.

"Grow up," spouted Dunkum. "You're rich compared to some kids."

"Yeah, kids in India, for starters!" Abby said.

Dunkum gave Abby a high five.

Jason made a face and scooped up a handful of wet snow.

*POW!*

He threw the snowball hard.

Dunkum dodged out of the way, laughing.

*Br-r-i-i-ing!* The recess bell rang.

"What'll we do about the fort?" Dunkum said. It was only half finished.

"We'll work on it later," Eric said.

The Cul-de-sac Kids agreed and ran toward the school.

Dunkum didn't line up right away. He checked out the fort. It was really cool. It had a large main entrance, curved like a

20

cave. There were lookout holes on the top and sides.

Making the fort with his friends gave him a good feeling. Abby would call it double dabble good.

But he didn't feel so great about something else. Miss Hershey's house.

Was it *really* haunted?

# THREE

Lunch recess came fast.

The Cul-de-sac Kids crawled around inside the snow fort. "This is better than making a snowman," Eric said. "And we've made lots of them."

Dunkum wasn't interested in a snowman. Something else was on his mind: the teacher's cats. "What's with Miss Hershey's cats? Why so many?" he asked.

Abby looked surprised. "She loves them, that's why."

"But eight cats? C'mon!" Dunkum answered.

23

"That's way too many," said Eric.

Jason was nodding his head. "I heard she willed her mansion to them."

"What's that mean?" Dunkum asked.

Abby spoke up. "When she dies, her cats get the house."

Dunkum couldn't believe his ears! He'd heard of fat cats, but *rich* cats?

Abby giggled. "They're like her children, I guess."

Dunkum shook his head. "Aren't *we* her children? Well, you know . . ."

Jason started jigging inside the snow fort. "Mama Hershey . . . Mama Hershey," he chanted.

The kids laughed, holding their stomaches. "You're crazy, Jason Birchall," shouted Eric.

Dunkum thought the same thing. Jason *was* a little crazy.

Finally, Stacy told Jason to quit dancing. "It's too crowded in here. Go outside and do your jig."

But Jason wouldn't listen. He kept it up. "Just wait'll tonight," he said in a weird voice. "Miss Hershey's house will be dark as midnight. There's no streetlights out there in the country. There'll be spooky music, too."

Eric joined in. "And don't forget all those cats." He and Jason were cackling like hens.

"Cats don't scare me," said Dunkum.

"What about *black* ones?" Jason joked. "How'd ya like a sleep-over with eight black cats?"

Abby put a stop to it. "Nobody knows what color Miss Hershey's cats are. It doesn't really matter anyway."

"Abby's right," said Eric. "But what about the bathroom? What color is *that*?"

Eric, Abby, and Stacy started laughing again.

"Hey! What's so funny?" Dunkum asked. "Who says Miss Hershey even *has* a bathroom?"

"Yeah, who says?" Jason said.

Abby waved her hands. "Whoa! Miss Hershey's a human being. People need bathrooms, right?"

Eric's eyes were wide. "But she's our teacher, so that makes her special. And different."

Jason stopped jigging. "Then maybe she *does* have a bathroom and wears pajamas . . . and takes out the trash."

"Well, why not?" said Abby.

Dunkum didn't want to hear about Miss Hershey's pj's or her garbage. He wanted to know if her house was haunted. And how she discovered music in Poe's poetry.

★  ★  ★

Dunkum's mom helped him roll up his sleeping bag. They tied it neatly.

"Don't forget your toothbrush," his mother said. "And your warmest pj's."

Dunkum remembered his flashlight.

27

He wanted to take it along for sure. "Anything else?" he asked.

His mother went down the teacher's checklist. "Let's see." Her finger slid over the page. "I think everything's packed now."

"It's just one night. I don't need much," Dunkum said.

His mother looked over the list again. "What about stuffed animals?" she asked. "It says you may bring two animals each."

Dunkum wondered about his friends. He'd heard Abby and Stacy talking. They were taking teddy bears. Two of the bears were going dressed as brides.

Dunkum had never seen a teddy bear in a bride's gown. *It's yucky girl stuff*, he thought.

"I'm leaving my stuffed animals home," he said. Dunkum couldn't imagine Eric taking stuffed animals.

But Jason Birchall? Well, maybe . . .

Lately, Jason had gone pet crazy. He

had a bunch of stuffed animals—snakes, lizards, and raccoons. Jason also had some strange real-life pets. Very strange.

Dunkum didn't want to think about Jason's bullfrog. And especially not Jason's tarantula! Why did people keep so many pets, anyway?

The thought of Miss Hershey's eight cats bugged him, too. But he pushed the pet thoughts aside. Nothing could spoil his reward. He had read twenty-five books and was going to his teacher's house!

Dunkum could almost taste the pizza. And the ice-cream sundaes. It was going to be a sleep-over to remember.

No matter what!

# FOUR

Miss Hershey's house sat high on a hill.

It didn't look like a mansion. Not a castle, either. But it was big . . . and old. Like a fairy tale house with a snowy roof.

"Wow!" Dunkum whispered.

His mother drove into the driveway.

Dunkum noticed tall trees along the road. And the icicles hanging from the porch. "What a cool place," he said.

"Sure is." His mom chuckled. "May *I* come to the sleep-over, too?" She was only teasing, of course.

*It's too pretty to be haunted*, Dunkum thought.

His eyes drifted over the area. A pair of stone lions caught his attention. They were statues, perched near the front door. One on each side.

"Hey! Look *there*," he said, pointing.

"Lions with full manes," his mother said. "I wonder where she bought them."

Dunkum stared at the lions. He didn't care about their manes or where his teacher had found them. He was looking at their mouths. They were closed!

*Good*, he thought. *These lions aren't scary.*

But it was daylight. Things always looked better in the light.

"You're going to have a great time," his mother said.

Dunkum waved good-bye. "See ya tomorrow!"

★ ★ ★

"Welcome," Miss Hershey said at the door.

"Thank you," Dunkum replied. He glanced at the lion statues once more and went inside.

Abby and Stacy were there. They were sitting near a lamp with fringes. Dunkum had never seen a lampshade like that. *Must be old*, he thought.

Jason and Eric were beside the hearth. The flames in the fireplace were snapping. Jason gave Dunkum a high five. "About time you showed up!" Jason said.

"The roads were a little slick," Dunkum said.

Miss Hershey nodded her head, smiling. "You all arrived safely," she said. "I'm so glad."

Dunkum sat down with Jason and Eric. He had a good feeling about this sleep-over. A *really* good feeling!

★ ★ ★

Milo had BIG ears for a cat. He was black with yellow slits for eyes.

"Say 'hello,' " Miss Hershey said to Milo. He was perched on her lap. He only blinked occasionally. And he looked upset. Was that a frown on his kitty face?

Dunkum didn't know exactly. He didn't care much for cats. Rabbits were *his* thing.

Milo's eyes made Dunkum shiver. What a creepy cat! Miss Hershey didn't seem to think so. She was hugging him and talking kitty talk. Or was it baby talk?

Dunkum couldn't be sure.

"Say 'hello' to the students," Miss Hershey told Milo.

After many pleas and some kitty kisses, Milo spoke.

It sounded like "Meow" to Dunkum. Nothing more.

Yet Miss Hershey kept fussing over Milo. That spoiled cat of hers.

"You're so-o-o wonderful, baby," she cooed.

Dunkum thought of his own pet, Blinkee. His poor bunny rabbit would not enjoy being around this many cats. Blinkee would've passed out by now. For sure!

Miss Hershey's pets turned out to be *four* cats. Not eight. Someone had stretched the truth. Times two.

So Milo had three little sisters. All fluffy black cats. They were Muffin, Minka, and Maggie Mae.

Muffin and Minka were OK names. But Dunkum wondered about Maggie Mae. Sounded to him like someone's great aunt.

★ ★ ★

Miss Hershey served up hot pizza. She made sundaes for everyone. Hot fudge, caramel, and strawberry.

The cats were stuck with tuna delight.

Dunkum wanted hot fudge *and* caramel topping. Both. Abby and Stacy had strawberry topping. Of course.

Eric asked for hot fudge. Jason, too, only he wasn't supposed to have chocolate. It made him jittery. He was having it anyway.

Dunkum glanced around. There were strange Old Mother Hubbard kitchen cupboards. Dark brown. The beamed ceiling was rusty brown. Same as the mantel over the fireplace. Even the hardwood floors were dull.

Dark wood. Black cats. Chocolate topping . . .

Was something scary inside those cupboards? What about the ceiling? Was something about to float down from the beams?

And the music? Abby was right about Mozart. Miss Hershey put on some violin music. Sounded like a mystery waiting to happen.

Miss Hershey's cats were almost finished with their dinner. Dunkum tried not to stare. They were going to have dessert now. They licked their chops and waited.

Milo stopped eating and glanced at Dunkum. Those orange-yellow eyes made him jumpy. Not jumpin' happy. No way!

Dunkum turned around. He saw more goodies coming. Miss Hershey was bringing a tray to the table. "Care for a brownie?" she asked.

"Thank you." Dunkum took a medium-sized one. They were extra dark. Extra chocolatey, too.

After supper, Miss Hershey began to light candles. Lots of them! There were candles in the windows and on the long mantel. Tall candlesticks on the grand piano.

"Will you play something for us?" Abby asked.

"Yes! Play the piano," Eric begged.

All the kids chimed in. "Please?"

"Very well," Miss Hershey said. She went to sit down. But there were no music books in sight.

"How's she gonna play?" Jason asked.

"Maybe she plays by ear," Dunkum replied.

Jason laughed. "How's she gonna see where to put it?"

That got everyone going. Even Miss Hershey was chuckling.

When things were quiet, she began. The melody seemed a bit gloomy. Dunkum thought so at first. But the more he listened, the more he liked it. Was it more Mozart?

Miss Hershey kept her hands on the piano keys afterward. The last notes were still sounding. Slowly, they faded away.

Then she lifted her hands. The piece was done.

Before the kids could clap, she began to speak. Her words were soft. "I'd like to recite a poem from memory. It's one of my very favorites."

*Uh-oh*, thought Dunkum. *Is this the bedtime story?*

" 'Once upon a midnight dreary,' " Miss Hershey began.

"It's from 'The Raven,' " whispered Abby.

Dunkum listened. He wouldn't let this raven poem shake him up. No way!

# FIVE

Miss Hershey continued. " 'Suddenly there came a tapping, as of someone gently rapping, rapping at my chamber door.' "

The poem excited Dunkum. Was it the flow of the words? Was it the air of mystery?

He really didn't know, but he liked it.

Miss Hershey went on. There was a *visitor* tapping at someone's bedroom door. " 'Only this and nothing more,' " said his teacher.

Suddenly, Dunkum felt something

behind him. He froze. Someone was tapping on his back!

He turned to see.

It was Milo. He was pawing at Dunkum.

*Kung fu kitty*, Dunkum thought.

He almost laughed out loud, but he didn't move.

Milo kept it up.

*What's he want?* Dunkum wondered.

Miss Hershey was still saying the poem. " 'Deep into that darkness peering . . .' "

It was hard to pay attention. A cat was pounding his fat paw on Dunkum's back.

Was Milo trying to say something? Maybe he had to go potty.

Dunkum didn't know what to do. So he raised his hand. Like in school.

Miss Hershey stopped. "Yes, Dunkum?"

"Uh, I think your cat needs something," he said. "Milo's scratching my back."

Stacy and Abby giggled.

Miss Hershey nodded. "Oh, Milo's just being friendly. He likes you, Dunkum."

*Great*, thought Dunkum. *I don't like* HIM*!*

"Now, where was I?" Miss Hershey said. She faced the students. "Does anyone feel a beat, a rhythm in this poem?"

Abby and Jason raised their hands.

*What's she mean?* Dunkum wondered. He didn't feel any beats. He only felt tapping, from Miss Hershey's cat!

"Listen now," his teacher said. She continued.

Soon she came to a familiar part. Dunkum knew he'd heard it somewhere. " ' 'Tis the wind and nothing more!' "

Milo continued his paw tapping. Dunkum wished the cat would back off! Be gone, with the wind, maybe?

When the poem was over, Dunkum

raised his hand again. "Sorry," he said when Miss Hershey called on him. "It's Milo—your cat—again."

"Is he bothering you, Dunkum?"

"Can you make him stop tapping me?" asked Dunkum.

Miss Hershey began to smile, then laugh. "Oh, Milo. Dear Milo," she said. "You've finally found the beat."

"The beat?" Dunkum muttered. "He's beating on *me*!"

Eric and Jason were snickering.

But Miss Hershey explained. "Milo's heard 'The Raven' many times. More times than I can count." She went over and picked up her fat cat. "That's wonderful, kitty," she cooed.

Dunkum thought of the repeated sentences. *'Tis the wind and nothing more. And . . . quoth the raven "Nevermore."* He felt a beat. Kinda. If Milo could feel it, maybe he should try, too.

Miss Hershey opened her poetry book.

She gave it to Dunkum. "Here, you read it," she said.

He began. " 'Once upon a midnight dreary, while I pondered, weak and weary...' "

Suddenly, he stopped. "Hey! I think I hear the beat," Dunkum said. "No, I can *feel* the beat!"

"That's very good." Miss Hershey seemed pleased.

But Dunkum had a question. "What does 'pondered' mean?"

His teacher explained. "To ponder means to think about something."

"Oh," said Dunkum. "I thought it meant to *pound* on someone!"

At that, Milo leaped toward Dunkum. The cat settled next to him.

Abby and Stacy giggled.

But Dunkum didn't laugh. He didn't know what to think. So he kept his eyes on Milo. And that swishy, bushy tail.

# SIX

Miss Hershey finished her talk about Poe, the poet. Her bedtime story wasn't so bad. Wasn't scary at all. Dunkum thought it was interesting. Really interesting. He'd learned something new. He'd found the music in a poem. Well, at least he'd found the beat.

Later, Eric and Jason wanted to check out the old house. They had an important mission in mind.

Miss Hershey gave the OK. "This house is an exciting place," she told them. "Look around as much as you like."

She headed to the kitchen to make hot cocoa. The *deep* chocolate kind.

Abby, Stacy, and another girl stayed in the living room. They were roasting marshmallows by the fire.

Two other classmates were playing board games.

Dunkum hurried to find Eric and Jason. They were upstairs, opening every door. "Hey! You guys are nosy!" Dunkum said.

Eric laughed. "We're just looking for the bathroom."

"I already told you. She probably doesn't have one," Dunkum insisted. "Remember, she's a *teacher*."

Jason jigged and jived.

"You had too much chocolate," Dunkum said.

"Wrong again!" Jason teased. "I need a bathroom."

Dunkum opened every door in the hallway. Even a broom closet.

Then . . . surprise! He found a walk-in closet.

He recognized certain clothes hanging there. "Look at this! I think I found Miss Hershey's closet."

Eric and Jason rushed over. "Let's see," said Eric.

"Any pj's?" Jason whispered.

"Are the clothes arranged from A to Z?" Eric teased.

"What about chalk? Or apples?" Jason said. "Maybe she stores apples for the teacher in there."

Dunkum turned around. "Stop it!" he said. He slammed the door behind him.

Jason frowned. "Wait! I was just getting started."

"I was afraid of that," Dunkum said. He shooed the boys back. "This is totally uncool. Miss Hershey oughta have some privacy."

Eric glanced at Jason. "Dunkum's right," he muttered.

But Jason dashed off. He darted here and there, looking for the bathroom.

Together they all searched. And found nothing.

Dunkum wasn't too surprised. "See? Told you!" he said. "Teachers don't have bathrooms!"

# SEVEN

Dunkum and Miss Hershey blew out the candles in the living room.

Soon, the lights were turned back on. "Who wants to play hide-and-seek?" asked Miss Hershey.

Abby and Stacy looked surprised. "*Here?* In your house?" Abby said.

"Absolutely! You'll discover some wonderful places to hide," the teacher said.

Dunkum looked around.

Uh-oh! Jason was missing.

Eric waved his hand up. "Can I be 'it' first?" he asked.

Stacy said, "Don't say 'can'—we know you can." She was always correcting speech. "You should say 'may I be *it* first?' "

Eric shrugged like he didn't care. "Well? Can I?"

Miss Hershey agreed. "But you must count to one hundred very slowly."

"Why?" Eric asked.

"Because there are eight of us hiding," she said.

"*You're* gonna hide?" Eric said.

Dunkum was surprised, too.

"I love playing games," Miss Hershey said. "I'm still a kid way down deep." She chuckled.

For a moment Dunkum believed her. He saw the wink of adventure in her eyes.

Just then Jason came downstairs. He was grinning.

"We're going to play hide-and-seek," Miss Hershey told him.

"Yes!" Jason said. He looked right at

Dunkum. "I know where *I'm* gonna hide!" And he disappeared again.

Eric began to count. "One . . . two . . . three . . . four . . ."

"Slow down," Miss Hershey said. "This is a very big house, you know."

Dunkum, Miss Hershey, and the others hurried to hide.

The sleep-over party was going great. So far!

★　★　★

Dunkum ended up in the library. He found a secret panel next to a set of encyclopedias. He leaned against the wall.

*Squeak!* The panel door opened.

"Hey, cool," he whispered.

Quietly, he crept in. It was dark as chocolate inside.

He sat on the floor and pulled the panel door shut. "Eric will never find me here," he said to himself.

He wondered if Miss Hershey knew about the wall panel. What a secret, *secret* place!

Slowly, he counted to one hundred. Just like Eric was downstairs. Counting might help pass the time. Because he didn't want to stay here too long. Not in this dark and dreary place behind the library wall.

Suddenly, he thought of the Poe poem. Miss Hershey's favorite. *Once upon a midnight dreary* . . .

Shivering, he wished he hadn't remembered. Not the gloomy midnight part. Not the raven part. This hiding place was way too creepy!

He waited a bit longer, listening. But he heard nothing. No sounds of Eric finding the others.

Nothing.

Maybe if he cracked the door, he'd hear better. Maybe even Eric's footsteps.

Dunkum listened longer.

Eric should be calling, "Coming, ready or not!" Surely by now.

Dunkum pulled on the panel door. It wouldn't move.

He pulled harder.

Stuck! It was honestly stuck.

Looking around was impossible. He couldn't even see his hand. And it was in front of his face! He knew it was because he bumped his own nose.

This time he jiggled the door. But it was jammed.

"Help!" Dunkum shouted. He called and called through the library wall. "I'm trapped! Somebody help me, please!"

# EIGHT

If Dunkum hadn't been so scared, he might've laughed. Here he was in the best hiding place of all.

Only *one* problem: it was too perfect. Hiding inside the wall meant Eric might never find him. Miss Hershey might not, either!

He kept calling.

He hollered.

He tried not to freak out.

If only Miss Hershey hadn't recited the poem. That raven poem. All of it seemed so spooky now. He wished he'd brought his flashlight up here.

He counted to one hundred again.

The waiting was getting boring. He yawned and leaned his head against the secret panel. He wished he were asleep in his own bed. . . .

★　★　★

Dunkum awoke with a start.

He heard pounding. "Dunkum? Are you in there?"

It was Miss Hershey!

"I can't open the door," he cried. "I'm stuck!"

"Don't worry, dear," his teacher said. "I'll get you out."

And she did.

*Click!*

The panel door opened and Dunkum crawled out.

"You're the winner, Dunkum! You fooled *all* of us," said Miss Hershey.

"Hoo-ray for Dunkum!" the kids shouted.

Abby and Jason were clapping.

"We thought we'd never find you," Eric said.

Dunkum was pleased. But he felt sorry, too. "I got a little carried away," he said.

Miss Hershey shook her head. "Oh no. Don't be sorry. I said this house was good for hide-and-seek. But I didn't think it would swallow you up."

"It sure did," Jason piped up. He went to the wall and pushed the secret panel. He made it open and close. "Check it out! Why didn't *I* find this place?"

The others took turns with the wall panel.

Finally, their teacher said, "It's very late. Did everyone bring a sleeping bag?"

"And stuffed animals!" Abby said.

Dunkum wished now he'd brought one. He followed the kids back downstairs. He whispered to Eric, "Did *you* bring a stuffed animal?"

" 'Course I did," Eric said. "Didn't you?"

"I thought only the girls would," replied Dunkum.

Abby pinched up her nose. "Not really. You should see the stuffed animals Jason brought. He's got a lizard and a—"

"OK, OK," Jason interrupted. "Just mind your own business, Abby!"

Dunkum wondered why Jason said that. Was he angry with Abby?

"It's almost midnight," Miss Hershey said. "Everyone's tired."

Dunkum wasn't. Not really. He'd snoozed for about half an hour inside the library wall.

"The living room will be the boys' bedroom," Miss Hershey told them. "Girls will sleep in the family room."

Dunkum rolled out his sleeping bag next to Jason. He found his toothbrush and flashlight. "Is there a bathroom after all?" he asked.

"Upstairs and three doors down," Jason said.

Dunkum remembered all those doors. "I thought that door led to a bedroom," he said.

"Nope, it leads to a huge bathroom," Jason said. He pushed up his glasses. "Yes, Dunkum, Miss Hershey *does* have a bathroom. She has three of them."

Dunkum nodded. "Guess that makes her a real human being, huh?"

"Three times over," Eric chimed in.

Dunkum wasn't surprised anymore. He'd learned some interesting things about his teacher. Miss Hershey was very cool. Cats or no cats!

Only cool teachers played hide-and-seek with their students. Only the coolest teachers said they had a kid's heart inside.

Dunkum chuckled. He'd been so foolish. It was silly to think this house was haunted.

Really silly!

# NINE

The living room was dark now.

All the boys were sound asleep. Except Dunkum. He was staring at the darkness. He couldn't get Poe's poem out of his head.

*Once upon a midnight dreary . . .*

He looked around the room. Eric was curled up in his sleeping bag. Two other boys were snoring. Jason was breathing loudly.

Just then Dunkum thought he heard a sound. It wasn't a snore or a loud breath. It was something else.

He listened hard till his ears hurt.

*Whooooooooooooooooosh!*

Was it the wind?

Dunkum couldn't be sure. Part of him wanted to get up. *Go look out the window*, he thought. Another part wanted to hide inside his sleeping bag.

He started to sit up.

*Whooooooooooooooooosh!*

There it was again!

Dunkum's hands were shaky. He found his flashlight and flicked it on.

Ah, much better. He shined it around the room.

Piles of sleeping bags were everywhere. He shined the light on the windows. Curtains leaned against the window frame like giants. Beyond them he saw the outline of the porch.

*Nothing to be afraid of*, he thought. Over and over he told himself.

The sound came again. It sounded like tapping. Was someone at the door?

He felt his muscles freeze. He pointed

his flashlight at the door. But the tapping changed places.

Quickly, he shined his flashlight on the wall.

Nothing there.

*Phooey.* He switched the flashlight off. *I'm not scared*, he told himself.

Then he saw it.

A shadow on the wall! A big black shadow.

*How can that be? It's dark*, he thought.

Dunkum felt his heart pounding. Still, he couldn't stop staring.

What *was* it?

He blinked his eyes shut. Then he opened them wide.

The shadow was a raven. The bird was huge. It had a long, scary beak and two skinny legs. And the body—the body was enormous.

It was just like Poe's raven.

Dunkum could hardly swallow. He was too scared to move.

Suddenly, the tapping stopped. The *whoooooooosh*ing stopped, too. And Dunkum heard only Jason's breathing.

"Hey, Jason," he whispered. "Wake up."

But Jason kept on sleeping. So Dunkum shook him. "There's a raven in the house," he said. Louder this time.

Jason popped up. "Wh-a-at?" He rubbed his eyes. "Where's a raven? I don't see anything."

"Look! Over there!" Dunkum pointed to the wall.

"Yikes! You're right!" Jason dove down inside his sleeping bag.

"Hey!" Dunkum leaned over and shook his friend. "You're no help."

Slowly, Jason slid back up. "You're not really scared, are you?" he asked.

"What do *you* think?" Dunkum said. "I'm so scared, I wanna go home." He meant it. "I'm gonna ask Miss Hershey to drive me home."

"In the middle of the night?" said Jason.

"Yes, right now!" Dunkum started to push himself out of his sleeping bag. "I'm not staying in this haunted house another minute."

Jason reached over and grabbed Dunkum's arm. "Wait. I have a better idea. Give me your flashlight."

Dunkum handed it over. "Here."

The boys got out of bed. They tiptoed to the window and looked out. It was snowing harder than ever.

"Guess you're stuck here," Jason said. "Looks like a blizzard to me."

Dunkum stared at the snow. He really wanted to go home!

Jason pulled on Dunkum's pj top. "Don't step on any bodies," he said, laughing.

"That's not funny," Dunkum said.

Jason turned and looked at the wall. "Whoa! It's gone," he said.

69

"What's gone?" asked Dunkum.

"Your raven," replied Jason.

Dunkum stared at the wall. The raven *was* gone!

"Maybe you were dreaming," Jason said.

"But you saw it, too," Dunkum reminded him.

"Oh, you're right." Jason started to laugh. "But I'm not half as scared as you."

Dunkum wondered why. His friend was being too brave!

Then . . . something moved. A black lump over in the corner, near the hallway.

Dunkum pointed. "Quick! Shine the flashlight!"

*Hisssssssssssssssssssssss!*

"What's that?" Dunkum asked.

"How should I know?" Jason said.

Dumkum wanted to run.

# TEN

"Who's there?" Dunkum whispered. "Who's hissing?"

Silence.

"Talk to us!" Jason said.

That's when Dunkum heard a new sound. A kitty-cat sound. "Mew."

It was Milo. Miss Hershey's fat black cat. His eyes looked like gold marbles.

The cat jumped over Eric's sleeping bag. Milo ran out of the living room. As he did, something big and floppy fell over.

Dunkum picked it up and ran to the hallway. There was a night-light lit near the floor. He held the floppy thing up to the dim light. "Hey, check it out," he said. "Someone brought Big Bird to the sleepover."

Jason started to push up his glasses. But they weren't on his nose. Then he coughed kinda funny.

"Wait a minute! This is *yours*, isn't it?" Dunkum said.

Jason shined the flashlight on his own face. He made a silly look and his voice squeaked. "Can't help I still like my Big Bird."

"But you were shy about it, weren't you? Isn't that why you wouldn't let Abby tell? Because *she* knew what stuffed animal you'd brought?" Dunkum said.

Jason didn't say anything. Probably because Big Bird was such a babyish thing.

So Dunkum dropped the subject. He wanted to check on something. He hurried to the living room and looked back at the hallway. He squinted at the night-light. He

got down on his hands and knees.

Yep. It was the right angle for a shadow.

Then he propped up Jason's stuffed animal. "Turn off the flashlight," Dunkum said. "Watch."

The boys stared at the wall.

"The shadow doesn't look like a raven *now*," Dunkum said. "Not at all."

He could hardly believe it. Had he only imagined the big black raven?

"Well, we solved that," Jason said. "But next time, remember what the Bible says about fear."

"Yeah, what?" asked Dunkum.

"When you're afraid, trust in God." Jason talked into the flashlight. Like it was a microphone. Like he was a preacher. "Please don't ask me what chapter or verse."

"Don't worry. I already know," Dunkum said. "It's in the Psalms."

"Cool!" said Jason. "Now let's get some Zzzzzzz's."

"Don't forget your Big Bird," teased Dunkum.

"He's a funny-looking raven," Jason said. He headed back to his sleeping bag.

But Dunkum stayed near the window. He watched the blizzard.

*Tap-a-tap tap.*

He wasn't afraid. "It's a tree blowing against the house," he said.

Dunkum heard another sound.

*Whoooooooooooooooosh!*

He punched the air with his fist. "'Tis the wind and nothing more," he said.

"Pssssst! Who are ya talking to?" Jason whispered across the room.

"Me, myself, and I," Dunkum replied.

"Just so it's not that raven," Jason joked.

Dunkum didn't laugh. He went over and crawled into his sleeping bag. "Thanks for reminding me. I forgot all about trusting God tonight."

Jason tossed his stuffed animal at

Dunkum. "Here, maybe this'll help you remember," he said.

Dunkum could feel the skinny legs and the long beak. Why'd he ever think Big Bird was a raven? "Silly me," he said. "This house isn't haunted. Never was."

"Huh?" said Jason.

"Oh, nothing," Dunkum replied. He peeked one eye open. He took one more look at the wall.

The night-light in the hall cast a shadow. But it was just a big, blobby shadow. Probably Miss Hershey's sleepy, fat cat. Nothing scary.

He turned over and hugged Jason's Big Bird.

*Zzzzzzzzzzzzzzzzzzzzzzzzzz!* Jason was already snoring.

"Sweet dreams," Dunkum said and smiled.

What a super sleep-over!

## THE CUL-DE-SAC KIDS

### Don't miss #18!

# THE GREAT TV TURN-OFF

It's "TV Turn-Off Week" all across America, and Eric Hagel decides that the Cul-de-sac Kids—their parents, too!—won't watch a speck of TV for the entire week.

All the kids agree. But what about the grown-ups? Can Eric and his friends convince the adults to go along with the plan?

Will it be a never-to-be-forgotten no-TV week? Or will the folks on Blossom Hill Lane be tempted by the tube?

# About the Author

Beverly Lewis remembers being afraid of the dark as a child. She would even hide under her covers at night. Once, her father told her something important about fear. "The Lord is always beside you—in the darkness, as well as in the daylight," he said. Beverly has never forgotten.

Jason's Bible verse in this story is Psalm 56:3. "When I am afraid, I will trust in you" (NIV).

Beverly thanks Peggy Littleton and her delightful students for the invitation to their real-life sleep-over. "I didn't see any ravens or hear any mystery poems," says Beverly. "But there was lots of laughter ... and food and fun." Congratulations to the CSCES L.E.A.D.E.R. readers!

# Series for Young Readers*
# From Bethany House Publishers

★ ★ ★

## THE ADVENTURES OF CALLIE ANN
### by Shannon Mason Leppard

Readers will giggle their way through the true-to-life escapades of Callie Ann Davies and her many North Carolina friends.

★ ★ ★

## BACKPACK MYSTERIES
### by Mary Carpenter Reid

This excitement-filled mystery series follows the mishaps and adventures of Steff and Paulie Larson as they strive to help often-eccentric relatives crack their toughest cases.

★ ★ ★

## THE CUL-DE-SAC KIDS
### by Beverly Lewis

Each story in this lighthearted series features the hilarious antics and predicaments of nine endearing boys and girls who live on Blossom Hill Lane.

★ ★ ★

## RUBY SLIPPERS SCHOOL
### by Stacy Towle Morgan

Join the fun as home-schoolers Hope and Annie Brown visit fascinating countries and meet inspiring Christians from around the world!

★ ★ ★

## THREE COUSINS DETECTIVE CLUB®
### by Elspeth Campbell Murphy

Famous detective cousins Timothy, Titus, and Sarah-Jane learn compelling Scripture-based truths while finding—and solving—intriguing mysteries.

* (ages 7–10)